CELESTE

A DAY IN THE PARK

CELESTE
A DAY in THE PARK

by martin matje

An Anne Schwartz Book

Atheneum Books for Young Readers

For my C.

Atheneum Books for Young Readers
An imprint of Simon & Schuster Children's Publishing Division
1230 Avenue of the Americas
New York, New York 10020

Book design by Martin Matje and Ann Bobco
The text of this book is set in Univers Extended.
The illustrations are rendered in gouache and watercolor.

First Edition
Printed in Hong Kong
10 9 8 7 6 5 4 3 2 1

Library of Congress Cataloging-in-Publication Data
Matje, Martin.
Celeste: a day in the park / by Martin Matje.—1st ed.
p. cm.
"An Anne Schwartz book."
Summary: When Celeste and her bear Tim go to have lunch at their favorite spot in the park, a duck steals their food.
ISBN 0-689-82100-X (alk. paper)
[1. Teddy bears—Fiction. 2. Toys—Fiction. 3. Ducks—Fiction.
4. Picnicking—Fiction.] I. Title.
PZ7.M4295Ch 1999
[E]—dc21
98-21628

Tim's real name is Timovitch Radetski.

But everybody likes to call him

← TIM.

Tim is a pet,

CELESTE'S PET,

and

they

are

very

good

Celeste and Tim

live together in

a very big city.

A very big,

very

NOISY

city!

One day, Tim says to Celeste, "Let's go somewhere."
"Where?" asks Celeste.
"To the park!" says Tim.

A PICNIC

in the park!!

It is a BRILLIANT idea.

That's why Tim is Celeste's best friend.

He always has such good ideas.

Celeste prepares a delicious picnic lunch. She makes some of her special cookies (crunchy peanut butter and smashed cornflakes), fresh marshmallow juice, and two large vanilla cucumber sandwiches.

Soon they are on their way to the park.

the reservoir
a bird

They go right to their
special spot. All around
it is calm, green,
and beautiful.
They are having a fine time.

Celeste begins
to eat her vanilla
cucumber sandwich.

BUT

in the middle of the lake,
someone else has noticed
Celeste's good-looking sandwich.

"Vanilla cucumber, that is one of my
favorite flavors," he quacks.

He swims over,

he climbs out,

and very, very
carefully, he
sneaks up.

Celeste begins to scream.

HIEF!

NOBODY eats my lunch except me!
NOT even one little nibble!!"

But the duck has already run off
with a delicious slice of cucumber.

"Come back here," cries Celeste.

And she runs after him.

Suddenly,

Celeste has bumped into
Police Officer Wallace B. Brekkit.

Officer,
Officer!
THEY
want
to
torture
me!

Celeste feels
very tiny.
She thinks of
three things that
she knows:

1. Tim is her very best friend.
2. She loves vanilla cucumber sandwiches.
3. You can fight a dishonest duck BUT you can't go up against

the **LAW** →

And
Wallace B. Brekkit
is the law.

Tim thinks it's time for him to help.

You can't behave like a spoiled duck, you know?

WE could be **VERY** good friends, you know?

Celeste is a VERY **NICE** girl, you know? And a very good cook too.

Just ask...

For example, what is YOUR favorite sandwich flavor?

"Now shake hands," Tim suggests.
"Ready, set, go!"
Everyone likes Tim's idea.

The next day, Celeste makes her special cookies, some watermelon cider, and

three huge chocolate and sausage sandwiches.

One is for Tim,

one is for herself,

and ONE is for . . .

Guess who?

THE
END?